PARIS

BY PHONE

Pamela Druckerman

illustrated by **Benjamin Chaud**

G. P. PUTNAM'S SONS

For Leila, Leo, Joey & Eve —P.D.

For my godmother, Ariane Adriani,
who introduced me to Paris —B.C.

G. P. Putnam's Sons
An imprint of Penguin Random House LLC, New York

Visit us online at penguinrandomhouse.com

Library of Congress Cataloging-in-Publication Data
Names: Druckerman, Pamela, author. | Chaud, Benjamin, illustrator.
Title: Paris by phone / Pamela Druckerman; illustrated by Benjamin Chaud.
Description: [First edition] | New York: G. P. Putnam's Sons,
an imprint of Penguin Random House LLC, 2021.
Summary: "When Josephine Harris follows her heart to Paris, she realizes that
the city of lights is still missing one thing—her mom"—Provided by publisher.
Identifiers: LCCN 2020009710 (print) | LCCN 2020009711 (ebook)
ISBN 9780399165061 (hardcover) | ISBN 9780525516736 (kindle edition)
ISBN 9780525516712 (ebook)
Subjects: LCSH: Mothers and daughters—Juvenile fiction.
Dreams—Juvenile fiction. | Paris (France)—Juvenile fiction.
Stories in rhyme. | CYAC: Stories in rhyme.
Mothers and daughters—Fiction. | Dreams—Fiction.
Paris (France)—Fiction. | France—Fiction. | LCGFT: Stories in rhyme.
Classification: LCC PZ8.3.D84 Par 2021 (print)
LCC PZ8.3.D84 (ebook) | DDC [E]—dc23
LC record available at https://lccn.loc.gov/2020009710
LC ebook record available at https://lccn.loc.gov/2020009711

Manufactured in China by RR Donnelley Asia Printing Solutions Ltd.
ISBN 9780399165061
10 9 8 7 6 5 4 3 2 1

Design by Nicole Rheingans
Text set in Bodoni Sans Text
The illustrations were done in gouache,
colored pencil, and gray pencil on paper.

Josephine Harris . . .
. . . really likes Paris.

"In France, the kids eat chocolate rolls
and take their poodles out for strolls.

"They stay up late to roast their snails
and send each other French emails."

At dinner, Jo says, "Mommy, please—
the French would never call this cheese.

"And really, Mother, what's the use
of life without some chocolate mousse?"

Her mom, who has a deadline soon,
says, "Josephine, go to your room!"

"Mommy, you're mean and you're not a good mother.
I'll pick up this phone and I'll find me another!"

The phone beeps and it rings,
it totters and tones.
It screeches and scratches
and rattles and moans.

Jo drifts off to a distant shore,
then hears a voice that says, "*Bonjour.*"

When she opens her eyes, she is in a new room
with an elegant lady who smells of perfume.

From the red of her lips to the beige of her sweater,
she's like Josephine's mother, but quite a bit better.

"Josephine, *ma chérie*,
we're so glad zat you've come.
My name iz Odile du Chateau
du French Bun.

"Let's get you dressed and
we'll go 'ave some fun."

A little boy who's named Pierre
gives Josephine a cold French stare.

"What are you doing
with my *mère*?"

"Pierre, be polite,
and get off ze bench.
Let's show Josephine
'ow to be French!

"A cat is a *chat*,
and no is *non*.

"'On y va' means
'Come on, let's go!'"

In gardens built for kings and queens,
French children jump on trampolines.

And when they're done, they shout, "*Encore!*"
(In French that means "We want some more!")

Josephine can't help but smile:
even the joggers run with style.

They look at art, then watch ballet,
and Jo receives her first *béret*.

"Odile, Pierre,
this is so cool,
but don't you go to work,
and school?"

"Welcome to ze nation
zat is always on vacation."

"To 'ave ze proper Paris day,
we must eat oysters in a café."

"Odile, *pardon*, I hate to be petty,
but could I please just have
some spaghetti?"

"To grow your
little appetite,
I do insist you
take a bite."

Jo loves the oyster,
it tastes like the sea.
Pierre says, "Now you're
French, like me!"

But Jo wishes that her mom could see.

Just then, Odile says,
"Look at ze hour!
We still 'ave time
for ze Eiffel Tower!"

"Ze perfect city, through and through.
It's obviously meant for you.

"Stay 'ere with Pierre and me.
You'll be so *chic*, so French, so free!

"All zat you need to say is *oui*!"

"Thank you for this Paris day,
but I don't think that I can stay.

"There's someplace else where I belong.
I miss my house, my room, my mom."

Jo gives Pierre and Odile a *bisou*
and tells the little cat, "*Adieu.*"

The phone crackles and crizzles
and sizzles and swups;
it guzzles and gizzles
and rizzles and rups.

As Jo's voyage starts to slow,
she wakes up to her mom's "Hello."

"In Paris I had my own brother, Pierre.
A trampoline sent us high in the air.

"I even had a real French *mère*.
The one thing wrong was you weren't there.

"Paris is perfect,
I hated to part,
but home is the place
they know you by heart."

**Though when she spots her phone,
Jo thinks:** *Next time, Rome!*

Le Lexique

adieu (ah-dii-uh)
  goodbye; farewell

béret (beh-ray)
  a round, flat hat

bisou (bee-zoo)
  a two-cheeked kiss

bonjour (bohn-juhr)
  hello; good day

chat (shah) cat

chic (sheek)
  stylish and elegant

encore (on-core) more; again

ma chérie (mah-sheh-ree)
  my sweet

mère (mehr—rhymes
  with "chair") mother

non (noh—rhymes with "go" but
  said through your nose) no

on y va (ohn-ii-vah) let's go

oui (wii) yes

pardon (pahr-dohn)
  excuse me